Date: 5/27/2011

BR HILLERT
Hillert, Margaret.
Dear dragon's day with father,

Dear Dragon's Day With Father

by Margaret Hillert
Illustrated by David Schimmell

NORWOOD HOUSE PRESS

DEAR CAREGIVER, The *Beginning-to-Read* series is a carefully written collection of readers, many of which you may remember from your own childhood. This book, *Dear Dragon's Day with Father*, was written over 30 years after the first *Dear Dragon* books were published. The *New Dear Dragon* series features the same elements of the earlier books, such as text comprised of common sight words. These sight words provide your child with ample practice reading the words that appear most frequently in written text. The many additional details in the pictures enhance the story and offer the opportunity for you to help your child expand oral language skills and develop comprehension.

Begin by reading the story to your child, followed by letting him or her read familiar words and soon your child will be able to read the story independently. At each step of the way, be sure to praise your reader's efforts to build his or her confidence as an independent reader. Discuss the pictures and encourage your child to make connections between the story and his or her own life. At the end of the story, you will find reading activities and a word list that will help your child practice and strengthen beginning reading skills.

Above all, the most important part of the reading experience is to have fun and enjoy it!

Shannon Cannon

Shannon Cannon,
Literacy Consultant

Norwood House Press • P.O. Box 316598 • Chicago, Illinois 60631
For more information about Norwood House Press please visit our website at *www.norwoodhousepress.com* or call 866-565-2900.

Text copyright ©2008 by Margaret Hillert. Illustrations and cover design copyright ©2008 by Norwood House Press, Inc. All rights reserved. No part of this book may be reproduced or utilized in any form or by any means without written permission from the publisher.
Designer: The Design Lab

LIBRARY OF CONGRESS CATALOGING-IN-PUBLICATION DATA

Hillert, Margaret.
  Dear dragon's day with father/ Margaret Hillert ; illustrated by David Schimmel.
      p. cm. – (A beginning-to-read book)
  Summary: "A boy and his pet dragon spend a day participating in activities with the boy's father"–Provided by publisher.
  ISBN-13: 978-1-59953-162-5 (library edition : alk. paper)
  ISBN-10: 1-59953-162-3 (library edition : alk. paper) [1.
Dragons–Fiction. 2. Fathers and sons–Fiction.] I. Schimmell, David, ill. II. Title.
PZ7.H558Ded 2008
[E]–dc22   2007036977

Manufactured in the United States of America

Father, Father.
Can you come here?
I have something for you.

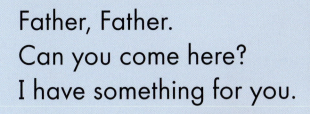

Here I am.
What do you have
for me?
I want to see it.

Oh, my.
How pretty it is.
I will put it on.
I like it.

It looks good on you.
And you are a good father.
You go to work for us.
Can we go to see where you work?

Yes, yes.
You can see where I work.

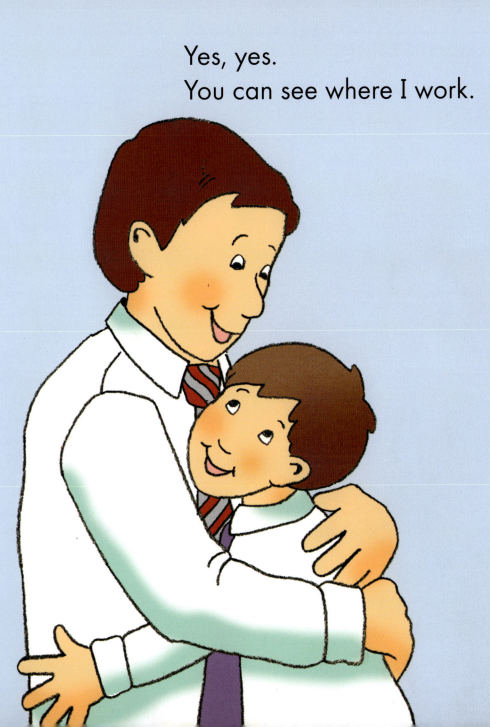

Can we get in the car?
Can we go now, Father?
Can we go to work with you?

Yes. Yes.
Get in. Get in.
Now we will go.

Away we go.
Away, away, away.

Here we are.
This is the spot.
Get out. Get out.
Here is where
Father works.

We have to go up.
Up, up, UP!

Look out here.
Oh, look out here.
Look way, way out.
What do you see?

14

And this is where you work?
It looks like a good spot.

Yes, this is where I work.
It is good to work
but it is good to have fun, too.
Now we can go somewhere
to have fun.

Here we are.
This is the spot.
Get out. Get out.

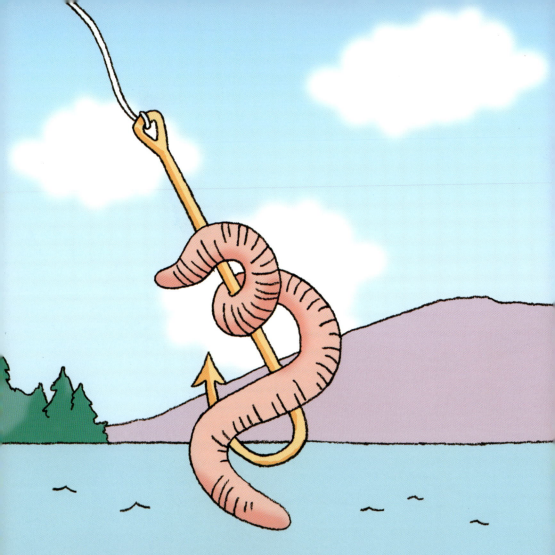

Put this down here.
Something will want it.
Something will come to eat it.

I see something.
Oh, oh, oh.
Look at that.

Look what I have.
Oh, look what I have.
It is a big one.

You have one, too.
And so do you.
That makes three.
One, two, three.

Now let them go.
We have to go.
Get in the car and we will go.

Here we are, Mother.
Here we are.
It was a good day.

That makes me happy.
Now we can make
something to eat.
That will be good.

Here you are with me.
And here I am with you.
Oh, what a happy day with Father,
dear dragon.

READING REINFORCEMENT

The following activities support the findings of the National Reading Panel that determined the most effective components for reading instruction are: Phonemic Awareness, Phonics, Vocabulary, Fluency, and Text Comprehension.

Phonemic Awareness: Rhyming Words

1. Say the following groups of three words and ask your child to tell you which two of the words rhyme:

cart, part, port	four, pair, stare	dirt, hurt, dart
bear, chair, bar	car, far, fur	core, care, store
park, dark, pork	skirt, start, shirt	shore, share, more

Phonics: r-controlled Vowels

1. Explain to your child that sometimes, the letter **r** after a vowel changes the sound of the vowel (for example, cat/cart).

2. Make four columns on a blank sheet of paper and label each with the following r-controlled vowel sample words: car, father, fork, air.

3. Write the following words on separate index cards:

far	work	horse	hair	barn	bird	north
care	jar	river	morning	bear	park	mother

4. Mix the cards up well. These lists are arranged according to vowel sounds to help you check the sorting activity that follows.

5. Ask your child to select a card. Read each word aloud or ask your child to read it and place the card under the word that represents the r-controlled vowel sound in the word.

Vocabulary: Story-related Words

1. Write the following words on sticky note paper and point to them as you read them to your child:

necktie   briefcase   skyscraper   elevator

2. Mix the words up. Say each word in random order and ask your child to point to the correct word as you say it.

3. Mix the words up and ask your child to read as many as he or she can.

4. Ask your child to place the sticky notes on the correct page for each word that describes something in the story.

5. Say the following sentences aloud and ask your child to point to the word that is described:

- Father carries important papers in his _____. (briefcase)

- Large cities have very tall buildings called _____. (skyscrapers)

- You need to ride an _____ to get to the top floors of a tall building. (elevator)

- Some people wear _____ when they go to work. (neckties)

Fluency: Choral Reading

1. Reread the story with your child at least two more times while your child tracks the print by running a finger under the words as they are read. Ask your child to read the words he or she knows with you.

2. Reread the story aloud together. Be careful to read at a rate that your child can keep up with.

3. Repeat choral reading and allow your child to be the lead reader and ask him or her to change from a whisper to a loud voice while you follow along and change your voice.

Text Comprehension: Discussion Time

1. To check comprehension, ask your child the following questions:

- Did father like the present the boy gave him? How do you know?

- What is father doing on page 9? Does he need those things for work? Why or why not?

- Why are the boy and the father wearing different clothes on pages 21-26?

- If you spent the day with an adult, what would you like to do? Why?

WORD LIST

***Dear Dragon's Day with Father* uses the 73 words listed below.**
This list can be used to practice reading the words that appear in the text. You may wish to write the words on index cards and use them to help your child build automatic word recognition. Regular practice with these words will enhance your child's fluency in reading connected text.

a	down	I	pretty	want
am	dragon	in	put	was
and		is		way
are	eat	it	see	we
at			so	what
away	Father	let	something	where
	for	like	somewhere	will
be	fun	look(s)	spot	with
big				work(s)
blue	get	make(s)	that	
but	go	me	the	yes
	good	Mother	them	you
can		my	this	
car	have		three	
come	happy	now	to	
	here		too	
day	how	oh	two	
dear		on		
do		one	up	
		out	us	

ABOUT THE AUTHOR Margaret Hillert has written over 80 books for children who are just learning to read. Her books have been translated into many different languages and over a million children throughout the world have read her books. She first started writing poetry as a child and has continued to write for children and adults throughout her life. A first grade teacher for 34 years, Margaret is now retired from teaching and lives in Michigan where she likes to write, take walks in the morning, and care for her three cats.

Photograph by Glenna Washburn

ABOUT THE ADVISER Shannon Cannon contributed the activities pages that appear in this book. Shannon serves as a literacy consultant and provides staff development to help improve reading instruction. She is a frequent presenter at educational conferences and workshops. Prior to this she worked as an elementary school teacher and as president of a curriculum publishing company.